# Squeakers

Written by: Stephen Cosgrove
Illustrated by: Robin James

A Serendipity™ Book

PRICE STERN SLOAN
Los Angeles

Copyright © 1987 by Price Stern Sloan, Inc.
Published by Price Stern Sloan, Inc.
360 North La Cienega Boulevard, Los Angeles, California 90048

ISBN: 0-8431-1442-8

20 19 18 17 16 15 14 13 12 11 10

Dedicated to Mike Farrell and his wondrous efforts to teach all children that someday in their lives they may have to say "NO!"

Throughout our dreams there are always hidden forests we have never seen before. Behind our fluttering eyes and that last, "But I'm not sleepy!" is a land of wondrous beauty. A place where anything can happen. A place now touched by a gentle breeze of imagination that ruffles the feathers and fur of all the creatures that live there.

And, oh, the creatures that lived there!: little, bubbly birds with feathers like eiderdown flitting about and chubby chipmunks chattering their days away. The squirrels were the most special of the animals. Squirrels with silver fur and almond eyes, and squirrels with almond fur and silver eyes. Squirrels that scampered this way and that looking for that certain, ripe berry. Squirrels that did nothing but sit on the wide branches and sniff the gentle breeze for some brief message of the season to come.

One of the many creatures that lived in the glen was a young squirrel named Squeakers. He had long, soft fur, gentle, velvet eyes and the most beautiful silver tail you have ever seen. When Squeakers wasn't doing his chores or learning his lessons, he would scamper this way and that, his fluffy tail floating behind him.

After playing all afternoon, Squeakers would sit patiently in the evening's hush as his mother combed the burrs and stickers from his fur coat and his long silver tail. She would comb and comb, chattering about his school, the meadow and all the things around them.

"Have you been doing your school work, Squeakers?" she would ask as she groomed him from head to toe.

"Yes, mother," he'd reply.

"Now you remember, Squeakers, always do what the elders say."

"I will, mother," he'd answer.

Early every morning, just after the dew had been painted by the morning sun, Squeakers would scamper off to school, his tail bobbing right behind him. He would run with the other squirrels and chipmunks to the old hollow log that served as school for all the meadow creatures.

They would sit as patiently as they could as their teacher, an old badger, taught them to add nuts and berries, and read all the signs that nature wrote in the forest. Squeakers, like all the rest, would concentrate as hard as he could as he sat with his soft, furry tail wrapped around him.

Then, just when he thought that he could learn no more, the blue jay would squawk loud and clear, and school would be over for another day. Squeakers would dash back to the meadow as fast as he could so that he could do his chores and be free to play.

One day, as Squeakers walked gaily along, he was nearly startled out of his wits by a voice from behind him. He quickly whirled around to find one of his neighbors, Mr. Mole, standing beside him.

"How are you today, little squirrel?" asked Mr. Mole in a kindly voice.

"I'm fine!" called Squeakers as he continued on his way.

"What's the hurry, Squeakers?" asked Mr. Mole. "Why don't you stay and share a hazel nut with me?" And with that, he produced a handful of nuts that looked, oh, so very good.

"Well. . ." said Squeakers, "my mother told me to come right home after school. Besides, I'm not supposed to take things from anyone I don't know very well."

"But Squeakers, you know me!" said the mole. "You go by my nest every day on your way home from school. I'll tell you what, you don't have to *take* the nuts from me. You and I can trade!"

"What do you mean?" asked Squeakers.

"Well, I'll give you some of these delicious nuts and you can give me a tiny bit of fur from your silver tail to use in my nest."

Squeakers thought and thought. The hazel nuts looked so good, and all the mole wanted to trade for was just a bit of fur. Why, he lost a bit of fur every time his mother combed his tail before he went to bed! And after all, the mole was an elder, and his mother had always told him to listen to his elders.

"I guess it's okay!" said Squeakers, and he took the offered nuts.

He had just bitten into his second nut when the mole yanked a whole handful of fur from his tail.

The mole stood there with the strands of Squeaker's silver fur held in his fingers. "Remember, little squirrel, don't tell anyone about this! It will be our little secret," and with that he slipped into the brambles and disappeared.

Squeakers slowly ate the rest of the nuts as he stared at his poor silver tail. The nuts were sweet, but now they didn't taste very good at all. A small tear worked its way down Squeakers' cheek.

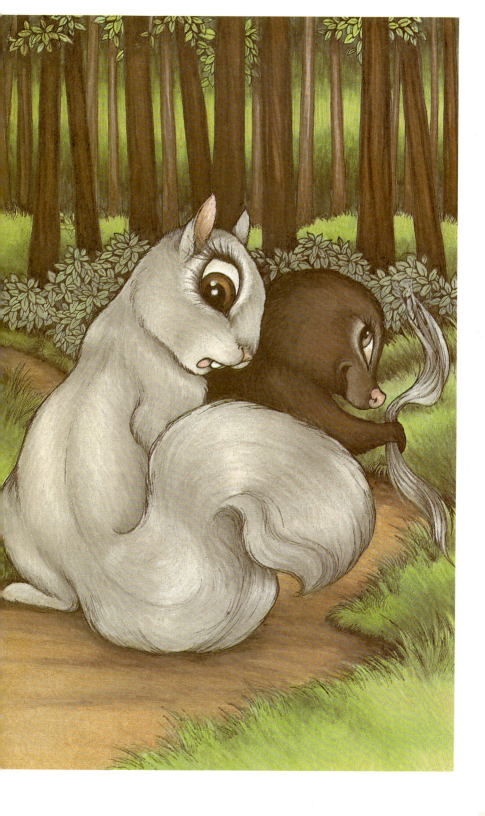

Squeakers arrived home, but he didn't feel much like doing his chores or playing. Instead, he quietly washed up and went to bed.

It wasn't long before his mother looked in and said, "Squeakers, are you all right?"

"Yes, Mother!" Squeakers answered quietly and quickly turned away.

His mother felt his brow, took his pulse, and did all those other things mothers do when they want to make their children feel much better. But this time it didn't help at all, and Squeakers fell into a dream-tossed sleep filled with mystery, mice and moles.

All during school the next day Squeakers sat on his log and dreaded his walk home in the afternoon. Several times when his teacher called on him to answer simple questions, he had to be nudged by a squirrel on his left or a squirrel on his right.

When the blue jay squawked to signal school's close, Squeakers dillied and dallied. Eventually, though, he was shooed from school and had to start down the path to his home. He promised himself that he would never talk to Mr. Mole again, but as he hurried on his way he heard a "Hello Squeakers! Where are you going?" from the bushes outside Mr. Mole's nest.

"I'm going straight home!" said Squeakers in a squeaky voice.

"Oh! I see!" said Mr. Mole as he coughed into his dusty hand. "Don't you want to trade with your old friend anymore?"

"Well..." stuttered a frightened Squeakers, "I...uh..."

"Look, little squirrel," he said as he steered Squeakers off the path and into his yard, "I not only brought nuts this time, but berries too!" He opened his paw to reveal some deep purple berries mixed with some sweet hazel nuts.

Squeakers was scared of the mole, but he didn't know what to do. "Well, this is the last time, but okay," said Squeakers as he took the nuts and berries. Then the mole grabbed a great fistful of hair from the little squirrel's tail. "Now, remember, don't tell! This is just between you and me," said the mole as he climbed into his nest.

The hazel nuts didn't taste as nutty as they should have, and the berries were bittersweet. When he had eaten them all, Squeakers didn't feel at all well; in fact, he felt pretty badly.

The next day, Squeakers resolved to tell the mole that he didn't want to trade anymore. When school was over and everyone had dashed up the trail, Squeakers made his way slowly along, rehearsing what he was going to say. "Listen Mr. Mole...No, that isn't right," he said as he scrunched up his face in deep concentration. Squeakers was so lost in thought that he nearly jumped with fright when the old mole stepped from the bushes.

"Are you looking for me, Squeakers?" asked the mole.

"Uh, yes, mole. I mean, Mr. Mole, sir. I, well, uh, I was going to tell you that I don't want to trade anymore."

"This must be your lucky day, squirrel," said the mole, "because we aren't going to trade anymore. From now on I'll just take what I want!" Then he ripped out a big chunk of Squeakers' silver tail as the small squirrel began to cry.

"I'll see you here tomorrow. Don't be late!" Mr. Mole called as he walked away.

The little squirrel didn't know what to do as he stumbled down the trail to the center of the woods, so he scampered up his tree and crawled into bed.

That night his mother and father came to his room and asked him what was wrong, but Squeakers couldn't bring himself to tell them what had happened.

"Son," said his father, "no matter what happened, we'll understand. But you have to tell us why you've been acting so strangely." Squeakers' mother put her arm around him to make the telling easier.

Finally, in a halting voice, Squeakers told them about the mole and the trades for nuts and berries. "I shouldn't have let Mr. Mole take fur from my tail, but he is an elder and I didn't know what to do!"

His parents listened intently. When Squeakers was finished, they said, "Your fur belongs to *you*. When anyone, anyone at all, wants to take or touch something that is part of you and you don't want them to, you tell them 'NO!' Then tell us about it right away. We're glad that you told us about Mr. Mole." Then they tried to hug away Squeakers' hurt and shame.

Soon afterwards the mole was banished from the woods forever. Everything returned to the way it was. The birds twittered in the trees and the squirrels raced and rushed about the meadow.

Everything returned to the way it was, and Squeakers returned to the happy squirrel he was, too. He would always remember that all you have to say is "NO!"

ALONG IN LIFE
AS YOU WILL GO
REMEMBER THE TIMES
WHEN YOU MUST SAY "NO!"

# Serendipity™ Books

**Written by Stephen Cosgrove**
**Illustrated by Robin James**

## Enjoy all the delightful books in the Serendipity Series:

| | |
|---|---|
| BANGALEE | LITTLE MOUSE ON THE PRAIRIE |
| BUTTERMILK | MAUI-MAUI |
| BUTTERMILK BEAR | MEMILY |
| CAP'N SMUDGE | MING LING |
| CATUNDRA | MINIKIN |
| CRABBY GABBY | MISTY MORGAN |
| CREOLE | MORGAN AND ME |
| CRICKLE-CRACK | MORGAN AND YEW |
| DRAGOLIN | MORGAN MINE |
| THE DREAM TREE | MORGAN MORNING |
| FANNY | THE MUFFIN MUNCHER |
| FEATHER FIN | MUMKIN |
| FLUTTERBY | NITTER PITTER |
| FLUTTERBY FLY | PERSNICKITY |
| GABBY | PISH POSH |
| GLITTERBY BABY | RAZ-MA-TAZ |
| THE GNOME FROM NOME | RHUBARB |
| GRAMPA-LOP | SASSAFRAS |
| HUCKLEBUG | SERENDIPITY |
| IN SEARCH OF THE SAVEOPOTOMAS | SHIMMEREE |
| JAKE O'SHAWNASEY | SNAFFLES |
| JINGLE BEAR | SNIFFLES |
| KARTUSCH | SQUEAKERS |
| KIYOMI | TEE-TEE |
| LEO THE LOP | TRAFALGAR TRUE |
| LEO THE LOP TAIL TWO | TRAPPER |
| LEO THE LOP TAIL THREE | WHEEDLE ON THE NEEDLE |

The above books, and many others, can be bought wherever books are sold, or may be ordered directly from the publisher.

### PRICE STERN SLOAN
360 North La Cienega Boulevard, Los Angeles, California 90048